The Thunderbolt Ball

The Thunderbolt Ball
and The Electric Paint

by Jerry Warner

illustrated by Don Silverstein

CYPRESS PUBLISHING CORP
Glendale, California 91204

Other Freddy Higginbottom stories:

The Wobbly-Wheeled Sputter Putter Popper

The Wind-Up Worm

The Super-Supersonic Cock-a-Doodle-Doo

The Skyrocket-Powered Chicken Hawk
   and The Impossible Sandwinkle Machine

The Crinkle Winkle Ray
   and The Chicken-Feathered Phantom
   and The Rocket Shoes

Production by David Charlsen & Others/Linda Gunnarson

Printed in the United States of America

International Standard Book Number: 0-89447-017-5
Library of Congress Catalog Card Number: 76-53181

The
Thunderbolt Ball

THE AIR OVER THE NORMAL SCHOOL football stadium crackled with the kind of supercharged excitement only the first football game of the season generates. Hundreds of hot dogs flowed into the fully packed stands, and rivers of soda pop went the same direction. Dogs howled to the music of the three-piece school band, which was made up of a skinny tuba-player, an off-key accordion-player, and a violin-player who had taken her first lesson that very morning. A squad of cheerleaders stumbled lamely on the sidelines in an effort to dance to the unsteady music of the struggling band.

After fifty-seven minutes of hard-fought, nose-to-nose, winner-take-all football, the scoreboard over the drinking fountain read: "Barker School Battling Baboons . . . 0, Normal School Thunder Chickens . . . 0." Excited throngs of ranting and raving football fans crammed the grandstands, rooting for their team to break the agonizing deadlock. The fidgeting football fans anxiously gazed at the lead-footed players staggering about the grassy gridiron.

With a mere three minutes left in the game, it was the Thunder Chickens' ball on the Battling Baboons' one-foot line. After a scoreless contest, the panting and dragging

1

Thunder Chickens could barely slouch into a huddle to plan the last play of the game. None of the players had enough energy left to crawl off the field and absolutely no hope at all of punching the ball that last foot over the goal line to win the hearts of all Thunder Chicken fans and eternal fame in the Normal School record books.

Freddy Higginbottom gallantly huddled his gasping and panting Thunder Chickens to ready the sagging team for its final plunge over the goal line. "Come on, Chickens!" he cheered. "Only one measly foot to go! Just twelve teeny inches! This time let's try the good old quarterback sneak play right up the middle! Remember, if we win this game, we go on to play for the county championship; so let's get fired up and blast those Baboons!"

Cassie Slapdash's rubbery legs buckled and she fell to her knees. "I'm seeing orange and green and purple spots in front of my bleary eyes!" she sputtered.

Charlie Stoots grabbed Cassie by her helmet and pulled her to her feet. "Purple-colored spots?" croaked Charlie. "That's funny. My spots are black and blue!"

Freddy rolled his eyes and continued his pep talk. "Now, gang, let's get out there and win this game for our parents, our fans, and grand old Normal School! Let's win this game for Coach Gonzales!"

Referee Wickett impatiently tooted his whistle. "You'd better break your huddle, Freddy. We can't keep these rabid football fans waiting all day," he grumbled.

Webster Lee fell backward out of the huddle and lay

flat on his back in the grass sound asleep. He began snoring like a buzz saw.

Freddy eyed the peacefully slumbering Webster and shook his head in disbelief. "How very, very embarrassing!" he sputtered. "Taking a nap at a time like this!"

Scarlet Rivera just shrugged. "Oh, let the little tyke snooze a while," she said.

The Thunder Chickens broke their huddle and slouched wearily to the goal line to face the growling and hissing Baboons.

The determined Quarterback Higginbottom pulled his helmet down low on his head. Charlie Stoots smeared glue on his fingertips, preparing to catch a pass.

"Come on, Chickens!" cheered Freddy. "Punch the ball in and we win!"

Scarlett smirked smugly at the leering Baboons. "We only have one foot to go! How can we miss?" she exclaimed.

"Scarlet!" roared Freddy. "If I've told you once, I've told you a million times, *never* wonder how we can miss! Whenever you wonder how we can miss, we always manage to miss!"

"Please, Freddy, hike the ball!" moaned Referee Wickett.

"HIKE!" bellowed Freddy.

The hiked football skittered between Freddy's legs and rolled crazily down the field toward the Thunder Chicken end zone.

The screeching Thunder Chickens and the howling Baboons charged down the field and dove headfirst after the fickle football. The slippery pigskin popped high into the air and bounced off Referee Wickett's head before sliding to a stop at Webster Lee's feet. The tiny Thunder Chicken gazed in awe at the precious ball and gulped.

"Webster! Pick up that pigskin and run with it!" roared Freddy.

Webster scooped up the ball and zigged and zagged down the field like a terrified rabbit.

"Go, Webster, go!" yelled the Thunder Chickens.

Midway down the grassy field Webster crashed head-on into a flying wedge of Battling Baboons and disappeared under a pile of thrashing and struggling football-players.

The bouncing football ricocheted off Coach Gonzales's nose and sailed lazily down the throat of the Normal School Band's tuba. The ball stuck tightly in the brass horn.

The surprised tuba-player sucked in a deep breath, crossed his eyes, and blasted out a note.

The awed Thunder Chickens and the open-mouthed Battling Baboons watched as the football popped out of the tuba and lazily fluttered over the crossbar on the Baboon goal posts.

Referee Wickett threw up his arms and shrilly tooted on his whistle. "Field goal for the Thunder Chickens!" he rasped.

"Bang!" went the final gun to end the seesaw contest. Hordes of cheering and howling Thunder Chicken fans poured onto the gridiron and carried the victorious players off the field on their shoulders.

The angry Baboon coach leaped off the bench and grabbed Referee Wickett by his whistle chain. "But it's not fair! We were beaten by an off-key tuba-player!" he bellowed.

"Sorry, but the game is over," replied Mr. Wickett crisply.

Coach Gonzales sat calmly on the sidelines, gazing at the empty football field.

Charlie Stoots pranced and danced about the grass. "We won!" he screeched. "The Thunder Chickens are champions of Middleville!"

Scarlet Rivera ripped off her Thunder Chicken helmet and slammed it down on the grass in disgust. "Champions, my foot!" she hollered. "We're all losers! We won, all right, but we're really losers!"

"But . . . but, Scarlet! We won the game!" squeaked Webster.

"Ha!" boomed Scarlet. "The Battling Baboons were beaten by a cross-eyed tuba-player!"

"True. Very true," admitted Freddy. "But the fact remains that we're still the champions of Middleville and must go on to play Turnertown for the county championship."

"We'll be pulverized!" said Cassie with a shudder.

"Perhaps," sighed Freddy. "But it's our duty to at least try to win. And maybe with a little luck we'll get through this season with our hides still on our backs!"

Freddy marched home under the gaze of admiring

football fans. Once he reached the Higginbottom house, he hurried upstairs to the electric room to continue his experiments with an exciting new way to cook gingersnaps.

At eight o'clock in the evening, Cassie Slapdash, the best detective in Middleville, wandered into Freddy's room and found the master gadget-maker perched atop a stack of electric wire by the window, tinkering with a small cannon-like contraption. Freddy aimed the strange-looking gun out the window and sighted down its TV-antenna barrel.

Cassie gazed through her magnifying glass at the peculiar gun covered with dials and gauges. "Ah-ha," she blurted in her best detective voice. "So you're at it again, eh, Freddy?"

"At *what* again?" asked Freddy, popping a flashlight battery into his latest invention.

Cassie removed her dark glasses and Sherlock Holmes hat. "Any good detective can see that you're puttering around with another one of your horrible electric thing-amabobs! Freddy, after Mr. Wrigglesworth caught his necktie in your Super Duper Lemon Squasher-Squisher and almost had his nose flattened permanently, I had hoped you would come to your senses and stop messing around with those disastrous devices."

"That was a close call, all right," agreed Freddy, bolting a coil of wire on the end of the TV-antenna barrel.

"What are you making now?" asked Cassie.

"Cassie, this clever piece of mechanical tomfoolery is a Genuine Gingerbread Ray Gun." Freddy twirled a dial on the bizarre gun.

Cassie scratched her head. "You mean it shoots gingerbread cookies?" she asked.

"Precisely!" proclaimed Freddy, popping open a lid on the Genuine Gingerbread Ray Gun. "This weird contraption will pop out the greatest gingersnaps ever made. All you do is dump a handful of goober peas into this container, lock the cap down tight, squeeze the trigger, and wham-bam-alaca-zam presto! Out the barrel sail piping hot gingersnaps!"

Cassie shivered. "You mean, wham-bam-alaca-zam *booooooom*! Out blazes a ball of fire and you burn down your room again!"

"Cassie," said Freddy, rolling his eyes, "have a little faith in me, will you? The Genuine Gingerbread Ray Gun won't explode."

Cassie frowned at the strange gun. "That's what you said about your automatic chicken-washer just before it blew that poor chicken of yours a thousand feet into the air."

"Accidents *will* happen," remarked Freddy.

"Accidents *always* happen when you fool around with your mechanical monsters," Cassie replied.

"Pass the goober peas, please," muttered Freddy coolly.

Cassie handed Freddy a handful of goober peas.

7

Freddy poured the peas into the Genuine Gingerbread Ray Gun and added a dash of chopped, luminous, wristwatch numerals, a pinch of paprika, a slosh of Tabasco sauce, a clove of garlic, a teaspoonful of ginger, and a pound of powdered candlewicks.

"All you'll get is a bellyache," warned Cassie.

Freddy smiled confidently, aimed the marvelous ray gun out the window, and started to squeeze the trigger.

"Wait!" shouted Cassie.

Freddy waited.

Cassie removed the mattress from Freddy's bed and rolled herself up in it like a frankfurter in a hot-dog bun. "When that goofy gadget blows the roof off the house, I'm not going with it," she declared. "You may fire when ready."

Freddy shrugged and squeezed the trigger on the ray gun.

Nothing happened.

"Whoops, I forgot to turn it on!" exclaimed Freddy, punching a button on the preposterous pistol. "And now, get ready to feast on a batch of fresh gingersnaps." Freddy squeezed the trigger.

"KA-BOOOOOM!" went the Genuine Gingerbread Ray Gun, and a dazzling bolt of lightning cracked out the barrel and streaked out the open window. The brilliant flash of super-light lit up all Middleville, and a booming thunderclap blew all the shingles off the Higginbottom roof. The blazing bolt blasted down Normal Street, mowed down three blocks of elm trees, chopped a fireplug cleanly in half,

8

and blew the tires off Officer O'Riley's squad car before slamming into City Hall and blowing the foundation out from under the tottering structure. Finally, the rumbling thunderclap boomed from mountain peak to mountain peak in the distance, and Middleville was once again quiet.

Cassie calmly unrolled the mattress and paddled out of the fishpond.

Still clutching the smoking ray gun, Freddy crawled from the petunia bed in the front yard and gazed up at the electric room, which stood open to the evening breeze, its outside wall curiously missing.

Cassie joined Freddy on the lawn and both watched as the ceiling caved in and the three remaining walls collapsed in a roar of splintering boards and crumbling plaster.

Freddy blinked his astounded eyes in disbelief. "I . . . I think I used a few too many goober peas," he stammered sheepishly.

Cassie clapped a hand to her forehead. "Well," she moaned, "instead of a batch of fresh gingersnaps, we got several blocks worth of elm trees, a fireplug, a squad car, and the foundation of City Hall."

"*And* my electric room," added Freddy meekly.

"Right," agreed Cassie. "Case closed!"

Ms. Higginbottom helped her gadget-making son dig out his prized electric possessions from under the rubble of the electric room. The two lugged the precious equipment out to Spiral's coop in the backyard, and Freddy moved in with his pet rooster.

Ms. Higginbottom carried the last suitcase crammed

9

full of light bulbs, batteries, and switches out to the coop. She tucked the suitcase under the roost and said, "Freddy, this is your third try at making gingersnaps this autumn, and this time you've roasted your room as well. I hope that living in a chicken house will teach you a lesson!"

"No more gingersnaps," promised Freddy, hanging his Thunder Chicken uniform on a hook over Spiral's water dish. "But living in a chicken coop really isn't so bad. I'll sweep out a few of the feathers and settle down comfortably for the rest of the autumn. And besides, I'm the only person in Middleville with a real rooster for an alarm clock!"

Ms. Higginbottom shook a finger at Freddy. "Your father, the firemen, and the police chief agree that if your room ever goes up in smoke again, you'll spend the rest of your life living with that chicken in this musty coop!"

"Yes, ma'am," replied Freddy, placing the goober-pea-powered thunderbolt-shooter on an apple crate beside his bed.

Ms. Higginbottom gazed over her glasses at the peculiar pea-shooter covered with dials and gauges. "What's that hunk of junk?" she asked.

"Only my goober-pea-powered thunderbolt-shooter," replied Freddy casually.

"*Thunderbolt-shooter*?" sputtered Ms. Higginbottom.

"Yes," declared Freddy brightly. "It shoots thunderbolts. I built it to make gingersnaps, but all it fires is thunderbolts. Would you care for a little demonstration?"

"No, thank you!" bellowed Ms. Higginbottom, scurrying for the safety of the house.

Freddy shrugged and continued to unpack his sooty belongings.

The very next morning, Freddy awoke at the crack of dawn with Spiral's first cock-a-doodle-doo. He scrambled into his Thunder Chicken uniform and polished the picture of a goggled chicken riding a rocket-powered egg painted on his helmet. This day was super-special, for it was the day of the big game against Turnertown. Freddy put on his helmet and was on his way out of the coop to go to football practice when the marvelous thunderbolt-shooter caught his eye. He stared at the dazzling device, and suddenly the most miraculous idea pinged and clattered and bonged inside his head.

With trembling fingers, Freddy carried his football and the goober-pea-powered thunderbolt-shooter outside to Spiral's pen. He poured a handful of goober peas into the gun along with a pound of powdered candlewicks, a pinch of paprika, and a slosh of Tabasco sauce, but decided to skip the ginger and garlic, fearing another super-thunderbolt. He stuffed the contraption up his sweatshirt sleeve, with only the tip of the barrel showing. He gulped, threw the football, and then pulled the trigger on the thunderbolt-shooter.

"KA-BOOOOOM!" went a rip-roaring bolt of lightning, and a Thunderbolt Ball blazed across the yard like a cannonball.

The ball whooshed across Normal Street, bounced off a power pole, skipped from rooftop to rooftop down the block, ricocheted off the fireplug on the corner, skimmed along the surface of Ms. Weems's fishpond, bounced off

11

Mailcarrier Chen's head, trimmed a foot of bricks off the Higginbottom chimney, and finally buried itself a foot deep in the lawn at Freddy's feet.

Freddy stood still for a full minute, gazing in awe at the smoking ball as it lay at the bottom of the crater in the lawn. He peeked up his sleeve at the goober-pea-powered thunderbolt-shooter, then shifted his gaze back to the cratered football. Suddenly he let out a whoop and danced merrily about the lawn, as thrilled as a miner who's just struck a mountain of gold. The flabbergasted quarterback of the Normal School Thunder Chickens realized that he had blundered onto a discovery that promised to add even more excitement to the game of football.

Quarterback Higginbottom quickly reloaded the thunderbolt-shooter, then rummaged about in the coop till he came up with three more footballs. He raced outside to the pen, hurled a forward pass, and clicked the trigger on the thunderbolt-shooter.

"KA-BOOOOOM!" roared the goober-pea-powered thunderbolt-shooter, and the earth under Freddy's feet rumbled and rocked. A brand-new Thunderbolt Ball whooshed high into the blue sky. Freddy shaded his eyes and watched the ball streak higher and higher and higher. He waited for the ball to come down. And waited some more. But the ball never came down.

"Whew! Too many goober peas!" gasped Freddy, reloading the goober-pea-powered thunderbolt-shooter.

"KA-BOOOOOM!" went the thunderbolt-shooter, and the next ball thunderclapped across the backyard and buried itself in a fig-tree trunk.

"Triple-wow! Those are powerful little peas!" exclaimed Freddy, reloading the thunderbolt shooter.

"KA-BOOOOOM!" went the thunderbolt-shooter, and another Thunderbolt Ball zoomed low over the chicken yard. Spiral squawked as shrilly as a tugboat whistle when the ball clipped off three of his tail feathers. The zipping ball rocketed down the sidewalk and struck Ms. Chen's mailbag, blowing a cloud of fluttering letters high over the treetops. Just before the mailwoman fell headfirst into the Higginbottom fishpond, she saw the Thunderbolt Ball clank off Tremblechin's tin-can head and sail high over the rooftops. The roaring ball popped the bulbs off a row of lampposts and finally slammed into a towering stack of egg crates that were being carted into the Middleville Market. With a roar of splintering crates and bursting cartons, ten thousand fresh chicken eggs blew high into the air over Main Street. Flying sheets of Grade A eggs rained down like hailstones all over town.

Spiral clucked his disgust at the messy matter.

Realizing the success of his outrageous invention, Freddy stuffed his pockets full of goober peas and hurried off to football practice.

Freddy was the last player to arrive at the Normal School practice field. Coach Gonzales squinted at his watch. "Try to get here on time, Freddy!" he barked. "After all, the championship is at stake, and you Thunder Chickens need all the practice you can get!"

"It seems to me that the Normal School Band's tuba-player should be out practicing, too!" whispered Scarlet.

Coach Gonzales gazed through his glasses at his motley players, who ranged in height from two feet, five inches tall to five feet, two inches tall. "As you know, men . . . uh . . . and women, the trick to winning at the great game of football is very simple: just get your sticky little fingers on that football and run as fast as a greyhound straight for the other team's goal line."

Freddy raised his hand.

"Yes, Quarterback Higginbottom?"

Freddy picked up a football and cocked his arm proudly. "I have a little surprise stuffed up my sleeve . . . ," he began.

"Nope! Nope! Nope! No passing this season, Freddy," interrupted Coach Gonzales. "Last year we threw the ball seventy-three times, and the other team picked it off *seventy-four* times. And let me tell you, *that* didn't look good when it hit the newspapers!"

"But, Mr. Gonzales," whined Freddy, "I have a whole pocketful of goober peas and . . . ."

"No peas, Freddy! Run with the ball today and eat your goober peas for dinner!" insisted the coach.

"Yessir," Freddy reluctantly replied.

As the morning wore on, the Thunder Chickens practiced running, tackling, punting, and picking themselves up out of the dust and dirt. At eleven o'clock, the frazzled football team flopped on the grass to listen to a final pre-game pep talk from Coach Gonzales.

The coach cocked his blue baseball cap to one side of his head and stepped before his sweating and panting team. "Ahem!" he boomed. "Needless to say, this is the day of the big game."

"Needless to say, we're going to be massacred," muttered Charlie.

The coach warmed up. "Today the hopes and dreams of our fans and the glory of Normal School will be riding on *your* shoulders."

The Thunder Chickens flinched.

The coach paced to and fro. "Now then, I want you to go out there this afternoon and win. Be courageous! Don't win for fame. Don't win for honor or glory. Win for me!"

The Thunder Chickens applauded the coach's speech.

The blushing coach bowed low and politely tipped his baseball cap.

Then the parched and panting Thunder Chickens staggered off the field and limped home.

By high noon, all Middleville was suffering from a bad case of frazzled nerves since everyone knew that only one team would emerge as champions of Middle County. Even Mayor Yakstopper was fussing and fuming in his office at City Hall. He realized that all the hopes of the proud Thunder Chickens rested squarely on the shoulders of Quarterback Freddy Higginbottom, so naturally he was nervous.

At ten past two in the afternoon, Freddy stuffed the

thunderbolt-shooter up his sweatshirt sleeve and stuffed his pockets full of goober peas. Then he tucked Spiral, who was official mascot of the Thunder Chickens, under one arm and set off for the football field.

A glorious, never-to-be-forgotten spectacle awaited Freddy at the field. A surging sea of screeching fans packed the stands to capacity. Brightly colored banners and streamers hung everywhere. The music of the raggedy band was breathtakingly off-key. Everyone in Middle County had come to see the greatest game of the year between the Turnertown Tiger Toads and the Normal School Thunder Chickens. The grassy stage was set for a dramatic exhibition of football at its grubbiest, noisiest, and craziest best.

Coach Gonzales sat on a bench on the sidelines, calmly munching on a piece of peanut brittle.

At one end of the Thunder Chicken bench sat Charlie Stoots, nervously waiting for the game to begin. Next to Charlie sat Freddy, slyly stuffing goober peas up his sleeve. Scarlet Rivera chewed an entire package of gum as she paced to and fro in front of the bench. Webster Lee, almost hidden from sight under his football helmet, glanced smugly across the field at the Tiger Toads. Carlyle Cornerstone lay sound asleep on the bench. Shooey Madera stuffed her thumbs in her ears to muffle the merciless music of the faltering band. Cassie Slapdash sat calmly polishing the chicken emblem on her helmet.

On the other side of the gridiron sat the terrible Tiger Toads, glaring across the field at the Thunder Chickens.

The glowering Toads intended to beat the Thunder Chickens by at least a hundred points.

Charlie Stoots fearfully gazed across the field at Henrietta Klink, the Tiger Toads' team captain. Henrietta was madly lifting barbells to loosen up her bulging muscles before the game began. Charlie's teeth clattered like a typewriter. "Fre-Freddy," he whispered.

"What?" Freddy whispered back, secretly checking the trigger on the thunderbolt-shooter tucked up his sleeve.

"How are we ever going to win this game playing against Henrietta Klink? We'll be lucky to get out of this with our lives! It should be against the law for a girl that big to play football. She weighs 175 pounds, stands nearly six feet tall, lifts weights, bends horseshoes, eats like an elephant, and roars like a lion."

Freddy nodded his head. "You forgot to add that Henrietta is also a karate champion," he muttered.

"I'm going home," groaned Charlie, leaping off the bench. "I forgot to feed my tropical fish."

Freddy grabbed Charlie by his sweatshirt and pulled him back. "Relax, Charlie," he said smugly. "I have a secret weapon up my sleeve that will really tickle the toes of the Tiger Toads."

Charlie's shoulders sagged. "Freddy, whatever you have up your sleeve had better be more powerful than a case of dynamite. Because if it isn't, we're going to wind up in Middleville Hospital."

Referee Rufus Wickett pranced to the center of the

17

field and tooted his whistle. "Will the team captains meet at the center of the field for the toss of the coin!" he boomed.

"Here we go," declared Freddy, sprinting to the center of the field.

The coin spun high in the air and the Tiger Toads won the toss.

Referee Wickett tooted his whistle. "The Thunder Chickens will kick off to the Tree Toads!" he bellowed.

Henrietta Klink picked up Mr. Wickett by the back of his shirt collar and lifted him a foot off the ground. Then she poked her big nose a half inch from the kicking referee's face and snarled, "It's *Tiger* Toads, not *Tree* Toads!"

Referee Wickett's face turned a bright shade of purple, and beads of sweat popped out on his brow. "Why, yes, Tiger Toads it is! And now, Henrietta dear, I must insist

that you put me down at once.''

Once safely back down on the ground, Mr. Wickett whipped out a handkerchief and mopped his brow. "Now shake hands and may the best team win," he croaked.

Henrietta grabbed Freddy's outstretched hand and shook Freddy like a rag doll.

"Ow! Ow! Ow!" roared Freddy, prancing about the grass, shaking his mashed fingers.

Mr. Wickett pulled Freddy aside. "Listen, Freddy," he whispered. "Just say the word and I'll call off this game on account of something or other. That girl is going to tear you limb from limb."

Freddy patted the thunderbolt-shooter up his sleeve. "No, thanks," he whispered back. "The Thunder Chickens will win this game with bravery, brains, and teamwork."

"I'll visit you at the hospital," whispered Mr. Wickett, tooting his whistle.

Coach Gonzales gazed calmly at the field.

Cassie Slapdash booted the ball high into the air, and the bruising battle was on.

Spiral let out a blasting cock-a-doodle-doo as the mighty Thunder Chickens charged down the field after the ball.

Henrietta deftly caught the spiraling football and stomped straight toward the Thunder Chicken goal line, with flying Thunder Chickens bouncing off her helmet as she went. Henrietta would have scored a touchdown easily had Charlie Stoots not courageously sacrificed himself. Charlie crossed his fingers, said a quick prayer, and fell directly in Henrietta's path. Henrietta tripped and fell with a resounding "whump" squarely on top of Charlie's head.

Charlie staggered to his feet and wobbled dizzily in a circle before falling backward off the field into the Thunder Chickens' water bucket.

While Charlie lay like a fallen statue on the sidelines, Webster Lee scampered onto the field to take Charlie's place.

"Come on, Thunder Chickens!" bellowed Mayor Yakstopper from the grandstands. "Let's get those Tiger Toads by the tail!"

"Cock-a-doodle-doo!" roared Spiral from his perch on the Thunder Chicken bench.

Coach Gonzales continued to stare calmly at the field.

The Tiger Toads broke their huddle and lined up nose to nose with the Thunder Chickens.

"HIKE!" boomed Henrietta, whose huge hands grabbed for the ball like swinging steam-shovel buckets.

But the football never reached Henrietta's outstretched hands. Tiny Webster Lee zipped between Henrietta and the ball and snatched the pigskin before it reached her.

Although Webster caught the ball, Henrietta caught Webster by his helmet. She roared like a lion as she punted Webster and the football high over the grassy field.

"MAAAAAAAA!" screamed Webster, flying high over the heads of the players below.

Freddy pranced and danced about the field under Webster and finally caught the soaring Thunder Chicken like an outfielder catches a fly ball.

Webster staggered from the field, and Charlie limped back on.

"It's the Thunder Chickens' ball on the Tiger Toads' forty-yard line!" declared Referee Wickett.

Freddy and the Thunder Chickens gathered in a huddle. "Now *we* have the ball!" exclaimed Freddy. "And for our first play, let's take Mr. Gonzales's advice and try the good old quarterback sneak play right up the middle."

The Thunder Chickens broke their huddle and lined up nose to nose with the growling and sputtering Tiger Toads.

"HIKE!" roared Freddy, and the ball zipped into his hands.

"Whump!" went Henrietta Klink on top of Freddy, driving the Thunder Chicken quarterback flat down on the grass.

The Thunder Chicken fans moaned and groaned.

Cassie and Charlie grabbed the limp Freddy by his ankles and dragged him back to the huddle. Scarlet gently slapped Freddy's face until his eyelids popped open.

"Okay, Freddy, so much for the coach's plan," said Scarlet. "What's next?"

Freddy staggered to his feet and shook his head to clear his foggy brain. "What's next is simple. Someone must throw himself or herself in front of Henrietta on every play. I can't play quarterback with a 175-pound karate champion driving me into the ground every time the ball is hiked. One more belt like that last one and I'll be finished for keeps. Now, do we have any volunteers to block Henrietta?" Freddy gazed at Charlie Stoots. "Charlie, *you* are elected."

Charlie's mouth dropped open. "*Me?*" he squawked. "But . . . but . . . but I'm too young to die! Henrietta will break my arms and my legs and all the rest of the bones in my body!"

Freddy patted Charlie on his helmet. "Charlie, it's for the good of the team. And for your gallant sacrifice, you'll get a Thunder Chicken medal," comforted Freddy.

"Close your eyes when she smashes into you and maybe it won't hurt so much," suggested Cassie.

Charlie's shoulders sagged. "You may send my medal

and my flowers to Middleville Hospital," he moaned.

The Thunder Chickens lined up nose to nose with the scowling Tiger Toads.

"HIKE!" bellowed Freddy. Then he cocked his arm to throw a Thunderbolt Ball.

The lionhearted Charlie closed his eyes and flung himself in the charging Henrietta's path. "NOOOOOOO!" screamed Charlie.

"Whump!" went Henrietta on top of Charlie.

Freddy threw the ball at Cassie Slapdash downfield.

"KA-BOOOOOM!" went the goober-pea-powered thunderbolt-shooter, and a Thunderbolt Ball blazed down the field. A roaring thunderclap blew the top row of fans backward out of the grandstands.

Cassie leaped high into the air for the blistering ball, but it whooshed over her outstretched fingers with a whistle and struck Mayor Yakstopper's top hat, blasting it to bits. A rolling clap of thunder shook all of Middleville, and thousands of pieces of blasted top hat fluttered down over the crowd like confetti.

The dumbfounded crowd sat stone still in the stands, and all eyes were glued on Freddy.

Referee Wickett raced into the stands and curiously examined the football. "Hmmmmmm . . . ," he muttered, "must be a powerful tail wind blowing to whip the ball about like that." Then he placed the ball back on the field and tooted his whistle.

Cassie and Webster pulled Charlie up from the grass and dragged him by his heels back to the huddle. "Is the game over yet?" sputtered Charlie.

"Not yet," replied Cassie. "We only have fifty or sixty more plays."

"I just wish she wouldn't roar like she does when she smashes me into the ground!" moaned Charlie.

The Thunder Chickens gathered around Freddy.

"Double-wow!" exclaimed Scarlet. "Freddy, throw another one of those dynamite balls!"

Freddy smirked smugly as he slyly slipped some more goober peas up his sleeve. "Smear lots of glue on your fingers because the rest of my passes are going to have lots of zip and zaz on them."

The Thunder Chickens guided the bewildered Charlie back to the line.

"HIKE!" roared Freddy.

"NOOOOOOOO!" screamed Charlie.

"Whump!" went Henrietta.

"KA-BOOOOOM!" roared a rolling thunderclap, and another Thunderbolt Ball ripped down the field.

The bug-eyed Tiger Toads, the Thunder Chickens, Referee Wickett, and the gaping fans watched the ball streak high into the sky. Even Spiral craned his neck to watch the ball soar higher and higher and higher. The zooming ball faded to a tiny dot, then disappeared altogether among the fluffy, white clouds.

"Astounding!" bellowed Referee Wickett.

The trembling Tiger Toads gazed in terror at Freddy.

The Thunder Chicken fans came to their senses with wild, howling cheers and thundering applause.

Freddy bowed low.

"Give the boy another ball and let's get on with the show!" shouted Mayor Yakstopper.

"Let's see another one of those jim-dandy rocket passes, Freddy!" shouted Ms. Higginbottom from the grandstands.

The dazzled referee placed another ball on the field and timidly tooted his whistle.

Coach Gonzales sat calmly gazing at the field.

Scarlet and Cassie dragged Charlie back to the huddle. Freddy secretly slipped more goober peas up his sleeve.

"Come on, Freddy!" bellowed Cassie. "Get those Thunderbolt Balls on target and we'll finish off the Tiger Toads for keeps!"

Freddy smiled confidently.

The Thunder Chickens again faced the wide-eyed Tiger Toads. Charlie bravely took his place on the line.

"HIKE!" roared Freddy.

"NOOOOOOOO!" screamed Charlie.

"Whump!" went Henrietta.

"KA-BOOOOOM!" went the thunderbolt-shooter, and a brand-new Thunderbolt Ball blazed down the field, conked Referee Wickett on the head, knocking him cold, and then smacked Cassie Slapdash squarely in her middle, carrying her over the field into the Tiger Toad end zone.

Referee Wickett regained his senses, raised his arms, and tooted on his whistle. "Touchdown for the Thunder Chickens!" he bellowed.

The Tiger Toad coach leaped off the bench and shouted, "Something very, very fishy is going on out there! Freddy's passes have some kind of weird whammy on them!"

"Play ball!" bellowed Referee Wickett, ignoring the coach.

Cassie and Scarlet dragged the sputtering and battleworn Charlie back to the line, and Webster kicked the ball for the extra point.

So, when Referee Wickett tooted his whistle a few minutes later to signal the end of the first half, the Thunder Chickens were in the lead by a score of 7–0.

Early in the second half of the game, Henrietta Klink came on like gangbusters and ran the football eighty yards in a spectacular touchdown play. And, as the Thunder Chickens watched helplessly, Henrietta effortlessly kicked the ball over the goal posts for the extra point.

With the score tied 7–7, morale was sinking on the Thunder Chicken bench. So when the Thunder Chickens regained possession of the ball late in the fourth quarter, Freddy decided he'd better give his team a pep talk to lift their sagging spirits. As he hollered and bounded about, though, the weight of the goober peas in his pocket caused the seam of the pocket to split.

Scarlet pointed at a river of goober peas streaming from the hole in Freddy's pocket. "Freddy, you're losing your marbles!" she laughed.

"Those are my goober peas!" wailed Freddy, frantically crawling around on the grass in search of the precious peas.

Referee Wickett gazed over at Freddy madly digging in the turf.

"I . . . I lost my goober peas," explained Freddy.

"Your *what*?" demanded Mr. Wickett.

"My goober peas."

The referee clapped a hand to his forehead. "Freddy, if it isn't asking too much, perhaps you might look for your goober peas *after* the game!"

"But . . . but I need those peas," insisted Freddy.

"After the game!" roared Mr. Wickett.

"Yessir," moaned Freddy, huddling his Thunder Chickens for the play. "I only have enough goober peas left for one last Thunderbolt Ball, so this last shot will have to be good."

"Let her fly!" exclaimed Cassie.

Freddy broke the huddle, and the two teams lined up nose to nose.

"HIKE!" roared Freddy.

Henrietta stomped around Charlie and leaped headfirst at Freddy.

"Oh, no!" whined Freddy.

"Whump!" went Henrietta, driving the quarterback into the grass.

The football fluttered high over the field, 'spun in midair for a moment, then sailed back down and plopped lightly into the hands of Charlie Stoots. Charlie stared in disbelief at the ball resting in his trembling hands.

Once, and only once, in every boy's life does such a shot at fame fall from out of the blue like a gift from the heavens. Naturally, Charlie couldn't quite believe his eyes.

"RUN, CHARLIE, RUN!" roared Freddy.

"RUN!" roared the Thunder Chicken fans from the stands.

Charlie pulled his dented and bashed helmet down low over his ears, gritted his teeth, and bravely raced down the field toward the goal line.

The roar of the crowd was sweet music in Charlie's ears as he dodged one flying tackler after another. It was a day at the carnival, winning all the marbles in one game, scoring "100" on an arithmetic test, and eating a whole gallon of chocolate ice cream—all rolled into one mad dash down the field!

A blur of flying tacklers whizzed all around Charlie as he scampered to within ten yards of the goal line. Charlie realized that fame would be his at last if he could just cross those final few yards. But out of the corner of one eye, he saw one last tackler between him and the beautiful end zone. Although the tackler swooped down on Charlie like a screaming eagle, Charlie was not to be robbed of his place in history—not *this* time. At the crucial moment he darted aside like a speedy rabbit, and the defender crashed helmet-first into the grass.

The roar of the crowd was earsplitting as Charlie proudly pranced into the wide-open end zone. Charlie's heart throbbed joyously and his eyes glowed with pride.

Coach Gonzales sat on the sidelines, calmly gazing at the football field.

Charlie danced a joyous jig around the goal posts, then turned around to receive the traditional pats on the back from his teammates and hysterical cheers from the crowd—but something was very, very wrong. Out of the corner of one eye he noticed something strange happening in the stands. Only the *Tiger Toad* fans were cheering and yelling and going wild, while the Thunder Chicken fans sat in a daze, their faces sullen. Charlie stared at the players on the field and gulped, for only the *Tiger Toads* were merrily dancing down the field toward him, and then the *Tiger Toads* were tackling him and shouting words of praise in his ear.

"Could it be that I . . . ," sputtered Charlie, already beginning to feel faint. Charlie started to feel queasy as he remembered that the tacklers chasing him down the field had *chickens* on their helmets, not toads!

Scarlet stomped up to Charlie in the end zone and glared like an angry gorilla. She pointed a finger at the opposite end of the field and muttered through clenched teeth, "That was a great run, Charlie, but the Tiger Toad goal is down there! This is *our* goal!"

Charlie was becoming dizzier by the minute. "Do you mean that I ran the wrong way?" he stammered, his rubbery knees already beginning to buckle.

"Yes, you bungling bumpkin!" roared Scarlet.

"Clunk!" went Charlie as he fell over backward in a cold faint.

"Touchback!" bellowed Referee Wickett, shaking his head. "Two points for the Tiger Toads."

Having broken the tie with only a few minutes left in the game, thanks to a good deal of help from Charlie Stoots, the smirking and jeering Tiger Toads kicked the ball off to the Thunder Chickens.

Scarlet caught the ball on the Thunder Chickens' twenty-yard line and was immediately buried under a monstrous pile of flying Tiger Toads.

Freddy huddled the gasping Thunder Chickens. "Listen carefully, everybody," he ordered. "There's only enough time left on the clock for one last play, so this will have to be good."

"What shall we do?" asked Webster.

Freddy stuffed his hands deep into his pockets and thought about the situation. Suddenly his eyes grew wide with surprise, and he yanked his hands from his pockets and opened a fist. Lying in Freddy's palm was a single goober pea. "I can throw one last Thunderbolt Ball!" he exclaimed, slipping the tiny pea up his sleeve.

The sweating Thunder Chickens broke the huddle and faced the snarling Tiger Toads for the last play of the game.

Cassie gulped.

"HIKE!" bellowed Freddy.

Charlie forgot all about blocking Henrietta Klink and sprinted madly down the field into the Tiger Toad end zone to wait for the Thunderbolt Ball.

"Whump!" went Henrietta on top of Freddy.

"KA-BOOOOOM!" went the goober-pea-powered thunderbolt-shooter, and a blazing Thunderbolt Ball skittered wildly down the field. The wayward rocket ball bounced off the top of Scarlet's helmet, tore Referee Wickett's shirt off his back, struck a cart loaded with popcorn bags, punched a gaping hole in the scoreboard, clipped the top off the flagpole, knocked over a row of cheerleaders, and trimmed the legs off the Tiger Toad bench.

The crazily bouncing ball left chaos behind it. Scarlet fell over backward like a falling tree, Referee Wickett raced off the field to get a fresh shirt, a shower of popcorn rained down all over the stadium, the flagpole fell over, and Tiger Toad players fell backward off their bench.

A squad of Tiger Toads scrambled after the wildly bouncing ball, their fingers frantically clutching for the great prize.

Charlie stood alone in the Tiger Toad end zone, gazing sorrowfully at the skittering ball that he knew would never come his way. Then he calmly closed his eyes and fell over backward in a tattered heap on the grass.

Meanwhile, the bouncing Thunderbolt Ball continued on its erratic course down the field. It shattered Coach

Gonzales's bag of peanut brittle, flipped over Shooey's outstretched hands, and was at last snatched from the grasp of a Tiger Toad by Cassie Slapdash.

Cassie tucked the ball under an arm and took a step toward the Tiger Toad goal, but ran headfirst into Henrietta Klink's helmet.

"Ooooooooofff!" bellowed Cassie, and the ball squirted high into the air over a sea of clutching fingers. The soaring ball drifted down into Henrietta's waiting hands.

The Tiger Toad fans went wild.

Henrietta stomped madly toward the Thunder Chicken end zone, sure of victory.

Out of nowhere came Webster Lee. He slipped under Henrietta's elbow and grabbed the ball from her big hands. Then he raced off in the opposite direction like a scared rabbit. Henrietta stopped short, searching her hands and arms for the missing ball.

Webster raced even faster.

Henrietta roared after Webster like an angry elephant and grabbed him by the tail of his sweatshirt. She cocked her throwing arm and hurled Webster and the ball in a whizzing bullet pass.

The crowd gasped as the dazed Thunder Chicken sailed high over the field.

Finally, Webster crash-landed on top of the Tiger Toad goal posts. The spiraling Thunderbolt Ball fluttered down, down, down and settled as lightly as a feather on top of Charlie Stoots, who lay slumbering peacefully in the Tiger Toad end zone.

Everyone in the stadium stared in shocked silence at the football resting innocently atop Charlie's chest.

Referee Wickett tooted his whistle. "Touchdown for the Thunder Chickens!" he bellowed.

"Bang!" went the final gun.

The crowd went wild. Thundering applause shook the stands and a sea of surging Thunder Chicken fans swarmed onto the field and carried the snoring Charlie Stoots off the field on their shoulders.

Coach Gonzales continued to gaze calmly at the empty football field.

And so ended what was perhaps the greatest football game ever played in Middleville. While Charlie Stoots became famous as the first football-player in history to catch a winning touchdown pass while asleep on his back in the end zone, Freddy Higginbottom limped home to the electric room to invent a pot of electric paint.

The
Electric
Paint

The
Magic Paint

ON AN EARLY SPRING EVENING, Mr. Higginbottom sat in the living room reading the evening paper while Ms. Higginbottom stood at the kitchen sink repotting a philodendron. Upstairs in Freddy's electric room, the light bulb over the worktable burned brightly, casting its brilliant rays on Freddy at one end of the table, thinking with all his mental might, and on Charlie Stoots at the other end of the table, buried in a towering stack of homework books. Charlie sputtered and moaned and mumbled and groaned and nervously chewed on his pencil eraser as he lost a pitched battle with homework problem number one in his arithmetic book.

Suddenly Freddy leaped from his chair and paced the floor with hands clasped firmly behind his back. "I'm going to try one last time," he announced.

"Huh?" sputtered Charlie from behind the arithmetic book.

"I'm going to have another crack at it," repeated Freddy.

Charlie raised his head slowly from his book. "Crack at what? Try what again?" he asked warily.

"At building a successful science-fair project," replied Freddy, wistfully gazing at the beaming bulb over the table.

"Oh, no!" wailed Charlie, turning slightly pale. "Please, Freddy, not *again*! Let's quit while we're behind. Your next project will probably level the whole town. And besides, my mother says that if one more of your gadgets blows up, I won't be allowed to set foot in this house ever again. She says your house is more dangerous than a cage full of starving tigers!"

Freddy stared at the light bulb. "How could anything else go wrong? We've already done all the damage we could possibly do."

"I'm not so sure of that—not while the house is still standing," sighed Charlie.

"Charlie! Where's your inventive spirit? Real scientists never call it quits after a few puny little failures. If at first you don't succeed—try, try again!"

"I wouldn't consider breaking all the glass in the state, or painting Middleville peppermint pink *small failures*," said Charlie, sinking low in his chair.

"We mustn't let a few petty misfortunes deter us from future success," said Freddy, staring with even more interest at the light bulb shining brightly over the worktable.

"Freddy, you talk about misfortune as if it were

nothing at all. You and I are lucky we aren't scraping pink paint for the rest of our lives or, worse, taking a very long vacation in the Middle County Jail. Once and for all, Freddy, count me out of your next science-fair project! I'll be satisfied with conquering the first homework problem in my arithmetic book.''

Freddy stared with fascination at the bulb over the table. "Charlie, we started the science-fair project together, and we'll finish the job together," he said firmly.

"All right! All right!" exclaimed Charlie. "Count me in. What's it going to be this time—an atomic bomb?"

Freddy continued to stare at the light bulb as though he were hypnotized by it, much as a moth flutters drunkenly about a flame. "I'm getting an idea," he muttered. "I definitely feel an idea coming on."

Charlie winced.

Suddenly Freddy's eyes brightened. Imaginary cogs and gears inside his head seemed to grate and clatter and screech as he hatched an idea to make a pot of electric paint. "Charlie!" he roared.

Charlie fell out of his chair to the floor.

Freddy pulled Charlie to his feet and pointed at the yellow bulb shining brightly over the table. "See that bulb?" exclaimed Freddy. "See it?"

Charlie looked curiously at the bulb. "I see it! I see it! But what's so great about a dumb old light bulb?"

"Plenty! Because we're going into the light-bulb business! My science-fair project is going to be a pot of electric paint. We'll mix up a batch of electric paint that will make things light up and shine. Why, rooms and buildings and clubhouses painted with the stuff will glow like neon lights, so nobody will need light bulbs or get electric bills from the power company!''

Charlie stared at Freddy blankly. He didn't have the foggiest idea what Freddy was babbling about, but he did know for certain that another one of Freddy's electric disasters was in the works, and his knees knocked at the very thought.

Charlie pointed a quivering finger at the Impossible Machine resting quietly in the closet. ''Why not enter that ghastly, impossible monster in the science fair and get rid of it?''

Freddy thought over Charlie's suggestion. ''No, the world still isn't ready for such a miracle,'' declared Freddy, closing the closet door. ''But the Impossible Machine will be of great value in making our electric paint.''

''Here we go again!'' moaned Charlie.

''This time nothing will go wrong,'' Freddy assured him, as he poked about the electric room in search of an empty paint bucket.

''Those were your exact words just before that delirious robot down in the garage painted the town pink!'' warned Charlie.

''You'll see! You'll see!'' proclaimed Freddy, as he pulled an empty paint bucket out from under a stack of wires in a corner of the electric room. He placed the dented old bucket on the worktable.

''If my mother finds out about this, she'll keep me

40

busy doing homework and mowing lawns from sunup to sundown for the next six years," groaned Charlie.

Freddy raced downstairs to the garage and soon reappeared in the electric room with a gallon jug full of liquid lightning left over from an earlier electrical escapade. He carefully poured every drop of the liquid into the bucket. "We begin mixing the electric paint with a gallon of freshly charged liquid lightning," he explained enthusiastically.

"That's certainly a beautiful beginning for a pot of electric paint," commented Charlie.

Freddy merrily dumped ten pounds of powdered magnets into the bucket. "After we mix all sorts of electric nonsense together, we'll run the bucket through the Impossible Machine to borrow some of the machine's glow power. Charlie, when this electric potion is finished, anything painted with the stuff will light up and shine just like a light bulb!"

"Or maybe blow up like a bomb!" exclaimed Charlie with a shudder.

"Don't worry, it won't explode," assured Freddy.

"That's what you said about the jet-propelled hockey puck just before it blew sky-high," said Charlie, pouring a cup of flash powder into the paint bucket.

"No problem! Whoever heard of a pot of paint exploding?" muttered Freddy, dumping a pound of glowworms into the bucket.

"Glowworms!" marveled Charlie, as he stirred the contents of the bucket. "This paint is really going to light up!"

Freddy raced downstairs to the kitchen and soon reappeared with a small jar the size of a soup can. Freddy pried the lid off the jar and emptied its contents into the bucket. "I bought this jar of pickled electric eel five months ago. I knew it would come in handy sooner or later."

Charlie cackled like a witch as he madly stirred the electric eel into the sticky paint.

Then Freddy pulled a piece of paper from his pocket, tore it into tiny pieces, and let the pieces flutter down into the pot. "For extra pizzazz, I just added this month's bill from the power company."

"That definitely adds style," agreed Charlie, stirring the gooey mixture.

Finally, Freddy dropped a flashlight battery into the bucket. "There—that should do it!" he declared.

"Actually," said Charlie, whipping the paint with the stirring stick, "making paint is fun. How could anything go wrong with a pot of paint?"

"Nothing bad will happen this time—absolutely nothing," promised Freddy.

Charlie peered down curiously into the pot of paint. "After all the troubles we've had with your gadgets, you really can't blame me for being a worrywart. But this time it looks like we've finally succeeded in making a harmless science-fair project."

Freddy stirred the pot of paint. "Hmmmmmmmmmm," he muttered, "the paint's still too lumpy—it needs more mixing. Help me carry it down to the kitchen."

Freddy and Charlie lugged the heavy bucket of electric paint downstairs to the kitchen table. Ms. Higginbottom stared over her glasses at the paint resting on the table. "Are you boys making a bucket of axle grease for the robot?" she asked.

"No, it's one gallon of electric paint," replied Freddy, pouring the contents of the bucket into his mother's food blender. Freddy clicked on the blender, which hummed and whined as it whipped the electric paint.

"How very, very interesting! How many electrics will a gallon cover?" asked Ms. Higginbottom, snooping into the blender.

"No! No! It doesn't cover electrics. It makes things light up and shine like light bulbs," explained Freddy.

Ms. Higginbottom frowned. "Well, please see to it that your rattletrap robot doesn't paint the town with it," she instructed.

"I'll see to it," promised Freddy, turning off the blender. He poured the paint back into the bucket and carefully washed out the blender.

Freddy and Charlie lugged their precious paint back upstairs to the electric room and carefully placed it on the center of the worktable. "The electric paint is almost finished," declared Freddy.

Charlie stirred the creamy paint with the mixing stick. "*Almost*? You mean it *isn't* ready yet?" he asked.

"Almost . . . . almost . . . . ," replied Freddy, opening wide the closet door to reveal the glowing, buzzing

Impossible Machine. "After we crank the bucket through the Impossible Machine to give the paint some extra glow power, we'll finally be ready to test it out on something."

"All right," sighed Charlie, "but I hope nothing goes wrong!"

"Everything will be fine! Just fine!" said Freddy, placing the bucket on the conveyor belt leading to the Impossible Machine's gaping mechanical mouth. He carefully checked the multicolored lights and intricate wads of wires on the flaming mechanical monster. "Everything seems to be in order," he declared.

Charlie crawled under the bed. "Go ahead and punch the start button, Freddy. I'll watch from here," came Charlie's trembling voice from under the bed.

Freddy donned a pair of sunglasses, crossed his fingers, and punched the start button on the Impossible Machine. Instantly, the marvelous machine surged into rhythmic motion. Cogs and gears raced faster and faster until the entire machine shook and rattled and worked up to a high-pitched wail. Lights on the machine flashed on and off, and the contraption glowed brighter and brighter until it blushed flaming crimson. The floor began to quiver and shake, and the entire Higginbottom house rocked on its foundation. The conveyor belt chugged as it carried the bucket of electric paint down the gaping mouth of the glaring monster. The marvelous machine glowed brighter and brighter until it glowed as brightly as the noonday sun. The sirenlike wail rose higher and higher, pictures fell from walls, and bits of plaster rained down from the ceiling like falling snowflakes.

"It's going to blow up!" exclaimed Charlie from under the bed.

But instead of blowing its top, the Impossible Machine quieted down like a tired giant lying down to sleep. The brilliant light waned weaker and weaker until it faded to the color of glowing embers. The high-pitched wail slowly softened to a quiet beeeeep, zuuuzzz, clack-a-ching-ching, and out the return chute rattled the finished bucket of electric paint.

Freddy placed the bucket on the worktable and examined it. The refined paint was as thick as cold maple syrup and the color of fried egg yolks, sunny-side up. Sparks flashed out of the bucket and popped in midair like a Fourth-of-July sparkler.

Charlie crawled out from under the bed and stood beside Freddy. Both boys peered into the popping pot of paint.

"The paint sputters and pops and flashes a lot more than I'd planned," stammered Freddy.

"Well, if you expect that sticky stuff to make things light up like light bulbs, it had better do a whole lot more than just lie there in that bucket like a dead fish!" exclaimed Charlie.

"Charlie, you're absolutely right," said Freddy, rubbing his hands together with glee. "Just wait till we paint something with it. Boy-oh-boy, will this house glow at night from now on!"

"Yeah, and we're going to win the top prize at the science fair with it, too," cheered Charlie, closing the closet door to cover the light beaming from the Impossible Machine.

"Just wait till Mr. Wrigglesworth gets a load of this stuff!" exclaimed Freddy, as he filled a tiny aspirin bottle with electric paint.

"Yeah! We'll sure light up Mr. Wrigglesworth's science class with that stuff," agreed Charlie.

Freddy squinted through his magnifying glass at the tiny bottle of yellow paint. "Once we've tested the paint, I'm going to paint the family car with it, paint Tremblechin, paint all the light bulbs in the house, spread a thick coat on the walls of the electric room, paint the lenses on all our flashlights, paint my flashbulbs, and instruct the power company to turn off our electricity.''

"And I'm going to paint my lawn mower and my bicycle and my tennis shoes and all the pages in my arithmetic book!'' exclaimed Charlie.

Freddy held the aspirin bottle high over his head. "The contents of this bottle will put an end to darkness forever,'' he proclaimed dramatically.

Charlie beamed. "And win us a medal at the science fair, too.''

Inside Freddy's closet the Impossible Machine glowed and rattled joyously. It merrily spun its cogs and gears and flushed proudly as it realized the remarkable power of the mysterious paint it had just made for Freddy Higginbottom.

Freddy raced downstairs with the bucket of paint. "Come on, Charlie!'' he hollered. "It's time to try out the paint!''

Charlie hesitated a moment, then raced out the door and down the stairs.

➷ 2 ➷

The
Baked Beans
Miracle

CHARLIE STOOTS AND FREDDY HIGGINBOTTOM lugged the precious pot of paint down to the kitchen to begin testing the paint's light-producing powers.

"The first-place award in the Middle County Science Fair is almost ours," declared Freddy, placing the bucket of egg-yolk-colored paint on the kitchen table.

Charlie rubbed his hands together impatiently. "Yep, this time the Higginbottom and Stoots inventing team will not fail," he said confidently.

"How can we possibly go wrong?" chuckled Freddy.

Charlie peered into the paint bucket. "Uh, how are we going to test this sludgy stuff?" he muttered.

Freddy opened the pantry door. "Testing is the easiest part of this project," he replied, rummaging among the stacks of canned fruits and vegetables.

"What are you looking for in there?" asked Charlie.

"Let me see here . . . . ," muttered Freddy, reading the labels on the cans, ". . . asparagus, sardines, okra, beets, lima beans, figs, baked beans . . . Aha! Baked beans! *Perfect*!" Freddy took the can of baked beans from the pantry and placed it on the table beside the bucket of electric paint.

"Baked beans?" exclaimed Charlie. "What are we going to do with a can of baked beans?"

"We're about to transform that can of beans into the most brilliant, eyeball-dazzling light bulb you can imagine—that's what!" declared Freddy.

Charlie scowled at the can of beans. "But *beans*? Why beans? A can of baked beans isn't very glamorous. How's it going to look in the history books? When our names go down in history for lighting the whole world, word will leak out that the first light bulb made with electric paint was a lousy can of beans!"

"If it makes you feel any better, Charlie, we'll say that the first bulb was made from a can of beans with franks. Okay? Does that suit you better?"

"Yeah, I guess so. The franks add a tiny touch of dignity to this ridiculous electrical caper."

Freddy disappeared into the garage and soon reappeared with a paintbrush. With the patience and skill of a great artist, he spread an even coat of paint on the can of baked beans until it was the color of fried egg yolks. Then he hammered a makeshift lid on the bucket.

Charlie examined the fresh coat of paint on the can. "The paint isn't glowing yet," he commented.

49

"The paint will glow after it dries. Believe me, once the paint's dry, that can of beans will shine like a floodlight," declared Freddy.

The two boys sat in chairs at the kitchen table impatiently waiting for the electric paint to dry. The only sound in the kitchen was the tick-tocking of the wall clock as it slowly signaled the passage of each and every second. After one full minute of waiting, Charlie squirmed and fidgeted and sighed with boredom. After five minutes, he leaped from his chair and, with hands clasped behind his back and chin lying on his chest, began to march back and forth across the kitchen in cadence with the ticking of the clock. Even Freddy was champing at the bit as they waited for the can of beans to light up and signal the success of their project.

After five more minutes of feverish pacing, Charlie suddenly blurted out, "I just can't stand it any longer!" and began blowing on the can and fanning it with his fingers to speed up the drying process. Freddy placed an electric fan on the table and turned it up to high speed to send a blast of air rushing over the can of beans. Charlie placed a heat lamp on the table and focused its rays on the can. "With the fan and heat lamp working together, the paint will dry in a jiffy," declared Charlie.

With the heat lamp blazing and the fan blowing up a storm, the coat of electric paint quickly began to dry. Freddy and Charlie scooted to the very edges of their chairs and sat with anxious faces just inches from the can of beans. They continued to stare unblinkingly at the big, yellow can.

"Shine, can, shine!" coaxed Charlie. "Glow, paint, glow!" chanted Freddy, cheering the paint on to shining victory.

Mr. Higginbottom wandered into the kitchen past the can-gazers to the refrigerator, where he fixed himself a salami sandwich. On the way back to his easy chair, he paused at the kitchen table to observe Freddy and Charlie huddled over the painted can of beans. "What's going on, boys?" he mumbled between bites of his sandwich.

"We're waiting for this can of baked beans to light up and shine like a floodlight," explained Charlie.

Mr. Higginbottom shook his bewildered head. "Schoolwork certainly has changed since I was a boy," he muttered, returning to his easy chair.

Charlie gingerly touched the painted can. "It's dry," he exclaimed, "but nothing has happened!"

Freddy touched the can. "The paint is still slightly damp. Let's give it a few more minutes."

Freddy and Charlie anxiously watched the unlit can of beans. Both inventors prayed for even so much as a twinkle from the electric paint, which was drying faster and faster under the heat lamp's blistering rays. After waiting three more minutes, Charlie banged his fist hard on the table. "It's another flop!" he hollered. "That electric slop didn't light up and shine. It didn't glow or flicker one bit. It hasn't even changed colors."

"The electric paint is another dismal failure all right," admitted Freddy. "But I wonder why it didn't work?" He shook his head sadly.

"That's easy to figure out," sighed Charlie. "It's just impossible to make a light bulb from a can of beans merely by sloshing it with a coat of egg-yolk-colored paint."

The defeated Freddy and Charlie stood up from the table with heavy hearts. As Freddy reached for the can to return it to the pantry, the can moved just a twitch. The movement caught Freddy's sharp eye. "Wait a minute, Charlie, let's give it just a little more time," he said. "Something may be about to happen."

"Only one minute more!" declared Charlie, plopping down in his chair again to watch the can of beans.

The can rested lightlessly on the table. Soon the electric paint dried completely, and instead of shining like a light bulb, the big can of baked beans slowly rose off the tabletop and hovered in midair! The can bobbed like a cork caught in a whirlpool as it drifted in circles nearly a foot above the table.

"Oh, wow!" gasped Freddy breathlessly.

"Nothing you make ever does what it's supposed to do!" sputtered Charlie.

The bedazzled boys stared open-mouthed as the airborne can drifted about over their heads. "Don't faint, Charlie. Whatever you do, just don't faint," whispered Freddy.

Charlie's eyes crossed at the sight of the bobbing can. "I wouldn't dream of it," he replied.

Freddy's jaw dropped open as the can of beans suddenly sailed across the kitchen and hovered over the kitchen sink. Then it drifted into the flow of air from the fan and was propelled back across the room, where it bounced off the refrigerator and shot toward the table, finally ricocheting off Charlie's dumbfounded head. The roaming can then bobbed into a stream of air from the furnace and was carried out the kitchen door, through the dining room, and into the living room, with the wide-eyed Freddy and Charlie staggering after it. Like a cork caught in the current of a lazy river, the renegade can of beans drifted across the room and settled like a fish bobber among the white clouds of pipe smoke hanging over Mr. Higginbottom's easy chair. Mr. Higginbottom remained engrossed in his newspaper, completely unaware of the can of baked beans floating over his head. Once again the can changed its course. It wandered around the ceiling light before cruising in a lazy circle about the living room. Then the dumbstruck boys watched as the wayward can of beans sailed back into the current of air from the furnace and zipped across the living room, through the dining room, and back into the kitchen.

"CATCH IT BEFORE IT GETS AWAY!" screamed Freddy, stumbling after the speeding can.

The goggle-eyed boys chased wildly after the fleeting can as it circled about the kitchen. Then Charlie made a flying leap at the soaring container. He missed and sailed headfirst into the pantry, raising an awful clatter.

Finally the big can of baked beans floated back into the current of air from the kitchen fan and shot straight at the open window, with Freddy's desperately clawing fingers close behind. With a "swish," the can darted out the open window and hovered over the fishpond.

Freddy and Charlie scrambled to the open window, stuck out their heads, and stared in astonishment as the can of beans soared in a lazy circle over the front lawn. "Tonight's supper just flew out the window," sputtered Freddy.

"Well, for gracious sakes!" exclaimed Ms. Higginbottom, staring over her glasses at the can of beans bobbing in midair over the lawn.

The bewildered boys rushed out of the house to the front lawn, where they peered with upturned faces at the floating can of beans.

Abruptly the big can of baked beans rose on an updraft of air and ascended high over the elm trees on Normal Street. It rose higher into the air above Middleville and soon faded to a tiny dot, then shrank to a teeny speck, and finally disappeared completely in the light blue, springtime sky.

Charlie gazed mournfully at the can of beans disappearing over the treetops. "We've done it again! Just another miserable failure!" he said glumly.

"That can is anything but a failure!" declared Freddy, whose eyes remained glued on the sky.

Charlie pointed a trembling finger toward the sky. "Freddy, you said that can of beans would light up and shine like a light bulb. The can that sailed away over the treetops didn't look anything like a light bulb to me."

"It's really a miracle!" stammered Freddy, gazing trancelike into the blue. "Now we're absolutely guaranteed to win the science fair!"

"Us? Win the science fair?" scoffed Charlie. "Mr. Wrigglesworth isn't going to be very impressed with a story about a can of baked beans that flew away."

Freddy didn't hear a word Charlie said. He fished the tiny bottle of electric paint out of his pocket and gazed at it as though it were more precious than diamonds. "I know it's impossible, but this fabulous paint frees whatever it touches from the force of gravity."

"Is that why the can of beans floated away like a balloon?" asked Charlie.

"Right!" roared Freddy. "This paint can release *any-thing* from the gravitational pull of the earth. Do you know what that means?" shouted Freddy, grasping Charlie's shoulders and shaking him joyously.

"That people will be able to fly about in the air like

birds and airplanes?'' stammered the rattled Charlie.

"More like balloons," cackled Freddy, jumping up and down with glee.

"Paint a coat of that stuff on me!" screeched Charlie. "I want to circle around City Hall and scare Mayor Yakstopper out of his wits."

"Oh, no! No! No!" cautioned Freddy. "No funny stuff until after we show this fabulous paint to Mr. Wrigglesworth."

"But Mr. Wrigglesworth will never believe our story about that flying can of beans," protested Charlie.

Freddy's face beamed with confidence. "Mr. Wrigglesworth will believe us after he sees the paint work for himself."

A frown furrowed Charlie's brow as he gazed solemnly at the bottle of paint resting in Freddy's palm. "Please, Freddy," he begged, "let's end this nonsense now, before we get ourselves into another mess of trouble. Why not bury that dangerous bucket of electric paint in the backyard and forget all about it before calamity strikes again?"

"Are you joking? You expect me to bury the greatest miracle to occur in the course of my experiments? No sirree! This little bottle of paint is priceless! It's perfectly safe, providing we don't accidentally get any on ourselves."

The front door popped open and Freddy's mother bustled down the porch steps to join the two boys on the front lawn. Ms. Higginbottom looked skyward, suspiciously eyeing the elm-tree branches. "Where's my can of baked beans?" she demanded, with one eyebrow raised.

"It went that-a-way," replied Charlie, pointing to an empty patch of sky directly overhead.

Ms. Higginbottom shaded her eyes and stared straight up into the sky. "I don't see it," she commented.

"I'm afraid the can of beans is gone for good," explained Freddy. "At this very moment the can is probably about two hundred miles out in space and traveling in the general direction of the moon."

Ms. Higginbottom blinked her astonished eyes and stared at the tiny bottle of paint. "Did that electric paint of yours send my can of beans flying way up there to who knows where?" she asked, pointing at the sky.

"Yes, ma'am. The paint frees whatever it touches from the force of gravity," explained Freddy.

"Well, fancy that!" cackled Ms. Higginbottom. "You've certainly concocted an unusual bottle of paint, Freddy dear, but you must promise not to send any more of my canned vegetables to the moon with it nor get any on yourself." She returned to her kitchen to send Tremblechin to the market for another can of beans.

Freddy and Charlie raced madly into the house and up the stairs to the electric room. Freddy placed the bucket of electric paint in the closet beside the happily buzzing Impossible Machine and closed the door.

"Now we have two monstrous miracles hidden in the closet," moaned Charlie. "Freddy, all I ask is that you be careful with that paint. Remember, just one slip, just one teensy-weensy accident with that paint, and it will send someone or something on a one-way trip into space."

"Stop worrying, Charlie. This time we have everything under control. Nothing can possibly go wrong. All we have to do to win the science fair is simply show the paint to Mr. Wrigglesworth at school tomorrow. After that, you can bet your life that the names of Freddy Higginbottom and Charlie Stoots will go down in history beside those of other great inventors like Thomas Edison and Benjamin Franklin!"

"But if anything goes wrong with that stuff, you can bet your tennis shoes that we'll be as infamous as Dr. Frankenstein!" groaned Charlie.

"Everything will turn out just fine," Freddy assured him. "At school tomorrow we'll succeed in amazing Mr. Wrigglesworth beyond his wildest dreams. That you can be certain of!"

↜ 3 ↝

A
Wild-Eyed
Flight

MONDAY MORNING BEGAN just like any other Monday morning in Middleville. The citizens awoke early and bustled about, dressing, cooking breakfast, and preparing themselves for a day of work or school. Everything was normal on sunny Normal Street. Mr. Murkywilk's milk truck buzzed from house to house as Mr. Murkywilk rushed up and down walks delivering fresh eggs, milk, and cottage cheese. A paperboy pedaling a bicycle loaded with newspapers wobbled down the sidewalk hurling a morning paper at every porch on Normal Street. At the Higginbottom house Spiral loosed a single, halfhearted cock-a-doodle-doo upon the world, then went back to sleep on his roost in the backyard coop.

For Freddy Higginbottom and Charlie Stoots this particular Monday morning was most important. It was the beginning of a day which hopefully would lead the two young inventors to their long-sought-after goal of completing a winning science-fair project. Freddy and Charlie bristled with enthusiasm as they prepared to show Mr. Wrigglesworth their extraordinary bottle of electric paint, and both boys were absolutely certain that success would be theirs at last.

Freddy dressed hurriedly, pausing only to dust off his tennis shoes and carefully stuff the tiny bottle of electric paint deep into a pocket of his jeans. He rushed downstairs to the breakfast table and gobbled down a bowl of cornflakes as fast as his spoon would fly.

Ms. Higginbottom frowned over her glasses at Freddy bolting the cornflakes. "What's the big hurry, Freddy?" she inquired. Ms. Higginbottom was alarmed at Freddy's unusual burst of Monday-morning energy, since he ordinarily needed ten minutes to poke downstairs, an hour or more to dawdle over breakfast, and five minutes just to get himself from the breakfast table to the front door.

"Can't be late for school this morning," blurted Freddy, leaping up from the table. "Got to get to Mr. Wrigglesworth's science class on time. Today Mr. Wrigglesworth is going to get the surprise of his life!"

Armed with the precious paint tucked safely in his pocket, Freddy burst out of the house and raced off wildly in the direction of Normal School as fast as his legs could carry him.

"Glory be!" exploded Ms. Higginbottom. "I can't imagine what's moving Freddy so fast on Monday morning, but I certainly hope it keeps up."

The puzzled Mr. Higginbottom shrugged. "I don't know what Freddy's up to at school, but I'm sure glad he's doing it there instead of here. One more of his explosions and this house would surely collapse!"

Freddy galloped down the sidewalk at top speed, his tennis shoes slapping rhythmically on the concrete. Soon another pair of tennis shoes thundered down the sidewalk as Charlie Stoots pulled up alongside Freddy.

"Good morning!" hollered Charlie. "How's the mad scientist of Normal Street this morning?"

"Just fine!" answered Freddy. "But I'll be a whole lot finer after we convince Mr. Wrigglesworth of the power of the electric paint."

"I'll say!" agreed the panting Charlie. "But if anything goes haywire with that paint in your pocket, I'll be leaving school twice as fast as I arrive."

"If anything goes wrong, it will be all Mr. Wrigglesworth's doing," assured Freddy.

Charlie huffed and puffed and gasped for breath. "Slow down, Freddy! I can't run as fast as I used to. Since September I've gained ten pounds eating Mr. Wrigglesworth's science demonstrations."

"So has every other kid in the class," chuckled Freddy.

"What do you suppose Mr. Wrigglesworth will produce this morning?" pondered Charlie.

"You can bet it will be something good to eat. I hope he turns out another batch of that luscious, nutty fudge he whipped up last week," replied Freddy.

"Yeah, Mr. Wrigglesworth certainly does turn out some masterful creations in that lab of his. My all-time favorite is his demonstration of how to grow yeast mold which ends up producing six dozen chocolate-chip cookies," said Charlie, his mouth watering.

"That's a classic Wrigglesworth science demonstration all right," agreed Freddy. "But I can't figure out how he does it week after week. Somehow those demonstrations of his always generate delicious pastries, tasty candies, savory bonbons, nutty nougats, rich cakes, and other terrific treats. The demonstration that most amazes me is the one in which he begins with a study of ocean water and ends up with a fresh batch of saltwater taffy."

"Absolutely brilliant!" agreed Charlie.

"And remember that spectacular experiment in which Mr. Wrigglesworth began studying a bullfrog under a magnifying glass and wound up with a whole platter of fried frog's legs?" asked Freddy.

"How could I possibly forget?" boomed Charlie. "After that incredible feast I decided to become a teacher. Watching Mr. Wrigglesworth conduct his demonstrations every week and come up with vanilla ice cream, cotton candy, cupcakes, and such has deeply inspired me to follow humbly in his footsteps."

"It's also made you fat," added Freddy.

"Fat, yes, but very happy!" chuckled Charlie.

Freddy and Charlie turned off Normal Street into the schoolyard and galloped down the walk past Principal

Torres, who was hoisting the flag up the flagpole. "Good morning to you, Ms. Torres," shouted Freddy and Charlie in unison as they thundered down the walk and disappeared among the school buildings.

Ms. Torres gazed curiously after the rushing boys. "Freddy Higginbottom and Charlie Stoots in a sweat to get to school on time?" stammered the principal, scratching her head in wonder. "Remarkable! In fact, it's almost frightening!" An uneasy feeling gripped the shuddering principal, who somehow sensed that strange and unknown events were about to happen at Normal School this particular Monday morning.

Freddy and Charlie rushed into Mr. Wrigglesworth's science class and plopped down in their seats just as the final bell signaled the beginning of the school day. Mr. Wrigglesworth stood in front of a long demonstration table at the head of the class, staring suspiciously over his spectacles at his two sweating, panting, and rasping students. "Congratulations, boys! It pleases me to have both of you here on time on Monday morning for the first time in over two years."

Charlie squirmed in his seat under Mr. Wrigglesworth's austere gaze. "Spring the paint on him and get it over with," whispered Charlie over his shoulder.

"Later!" whispered Freddy.

Mr. Wrigglesworth tapped a pointer on the tabletop to bring the class to order. "Ahem!" he boomed. "A most hearty good morning to all of you eager science students."

"Where are the eager ones?" whispered Charlie, glancing curiously about the classroom.

"Shhhhhhhh!" whispered Freddy.

"Ahem!" continued Mr. Wrigglesworth. "Today's science demonstration will cover the fascinating wildflowers of Timbuktu. But before I begin, does anyone have anything to share with the rest of the class?"

"I do! I do!" screeched Jamie Smith, springing from his seat.

"Do proceed, Jamie," encouraged Mr. Wrigglesworth.

Jamie scratched frantically at his itching arms and legs. "Yesterday I went on a picnic to Middle Park," he began, scratching even harder. "I made the most of the opportunity by searching for wildflowers to add to my collection for the science fair."

"And did you find any rare specimens to share with us?" inquired the beaming Wrigglesworth.

"Not even a single weed!" mumbled Jamie glumly. "All I could find was tons and tons of poison oak. But my little brother got his head stuck in a barbecue pit and the fire department had to come and dig him out," he offered hopefully.

"Fascinating!" snarled Mr. Wrigglesworth.

Freddy raised his hand.

Mr. Wrigglesworth opened a book of dried and pressed wildflowers. "And now, on to the wildflowers of . . . ."

Freddy waved his hand wildly in the air. "Mr. Wrigglesworth, I have something very important to share with the class.''

"Not now, Freddy, maybe tomorrow. I've had all the show-and-tell I can stand for one day," said Mr. Wrigglesworth, holding the pressed flowers high for all to see.

"But Mr. Wrigglesworth, I have something wonderful to show the class," persisted Freddy.

"Not now, Freddy!"

"But . . . ."

"Later, boy! Later! Can't you see I'm busy up here?"

"But I have something *outstanding* to show the class!" whined Freddy.

"OH, ALL RIGHT!" stormed Mr. Wrigglesworth. "GET ON WITH IT, THEN."

Freddy stood beside his desk. Slowly, with much drama and suspense, he pulled the tiny aspirin bottle from his pocket and held it high enough for all to see. Everyone in the classroom craned their necks and squinted curiously at the tiny bottle.

"What you're about to see and hear this morning will truly amaze you," began Freddy proudly. "You'll be shocked and awed by the magnificence of what is contained inside this tiny bottle."

"Get to the point, Freddy," muttered Mr. Wrigglesworth, impatiently tapping his pointer on the blackboard. "What's in that aspirin bottle?"

Charlie squirmed nervously in his seat.

"This is a bottle of electric paint," announced Freddy.

65

"Anything painted with this egg-yolk-colored pigment will be freed from the force of gravity and will soar through the air like a bird."

"How many birds have you painted with it?" scoffed Mr. Wrigglesworth.

The students chuckled.

"It really makes things fly," insisted Freddy. "If the custodian painted the school with this paint, why, the whole school would soar high into the air and float away like a blimp."

The students cackled and giggled even louder.

"Come now, Freddy!" protested Mr. Wrigglesworth. "We all know that it's impossible to make something fly merely by sloshing it with a dab of egg-yolk-colored paint."

The students laughed out loud.

Charlie Stoots slouched down in his seat.

"Well, this paint sent a can of baked beans to the moon," retorted Freddy.

"It was a can of baked beans with *franks*," corrected Charlie.

The students roared with laughter.

Mr. Wrigglesworth snatched the bottle of paint from Freddy. "HO! HO! HO!" he roared. "Look here. I'll just dab a bit of paint on my laboratory apron and then fly out the window. HAW! HAW!"

The students laughed hysterically. A few fell from

their chairs and rolled about the floor, holding their middles.

Charlie was speechless.

"Don't dab any of that paint on yourself," warned Freddy. "Please, Mr. Wrigglesworth, don't do it!"

Mr. Wrigglesworth removed the cap from the aspirin bottle and dabbed a spot of electric paint on his apron. "See?" exclaimed Mr. Wrigglesworth. "See, Freddy? I'm not flying around like a bird. Now you may sit down at your desk and save your tall tales for somebody who will believe them."

"But, Mr. Wrigglesworth, you've got to remove your apron before that paint dries!" pleaded Freddy.

"Freddy, that's enough nonsense!" ordered Mr. Wrigglesworth sternly.

"Yessir," replied Freddy with a shrug. "But be ready to grab something when you start to float away."

Mr. Wrigglesworth returned to the blackboard and continued his wildflower lecture.

Charlie's knees began to knock and beads of cold sweat popped out on his brow.

The electric paint dried slightly, and Mr. Wrigglesworth rose an inch off the floor.

Charlie eyed the classroom door, preparing to flee, but was too weak in the knees to rise from his chair.

The day was hot, and the spot of electric paint on Mr. Wrigglesworth's apron soon dried completely. The science teacher drifted up off the floor until his head collided with a light fixture on the ceiling.

"WHAT IS THIS?" shrieked Mr. Wrigglesworth. "HELP! SOMEBODY HELP! FREDDY, TURN OFF THE PAINT!"

"I can't!" screeched Freddy. He raced from his desk and grabbed Mr. Wrigglesworth's struggling legs.

"HEEEEELP!" shrieked Mr. Wrigglesworth, thrashing about and flailing his arms and legs in panic.

"I CAN'T HOLD ONTO YOUR LEGS WITH YOU THRASHING ABOUT SO!" exclaimed Freddy.

Charlie watched these goings-on in a growing state of helplessness as his body became numb all over.

Mr. Wrigglesworth drifted toward the open window.

"I TAKE IT BACK, FREDDY!" cried Mr. Wrigglesworth. "YOUR ELECTRIC PAINT REALLY WORKS! NOW THE JOKE IS OVER, SO GET ME DOWN!"

"I CAN'T HELP YOU IF YOU DON'T STOP THRASHING ABOUT!" replied Freddy.

The students sat frozen in their seats like plaster statues. Every mouth dropped open wide.

"CALL THE POLICE!" bellowed the wild-eyed Wrigglesworth. "NO, CALL THE AIR FORCE! CALL ANYBODY!"

Charlie fell from his seat flat on the floor in a stone-cold faint.

Mr. Wrigglesworth's head and shoulders drifted out the open window.

Freddy gripped the struggling science teacher's legs until Mr. Wrigglesworth's shoes popped off, and the poor teacher sailed out the window.

The students scrambled from their desks and pressed their faces against the windowpanes as they watched their bellowing teacher grab for the basketball hoop but miss it and rise up over the school buildings.

Freddy stuck his head out the window. "YOO HOO! MR. WRIGGLESWORTH! TAKE OFF YOUR APRON! IT'S YOUR ONLY CHANCE! TAKE OFF YOUR APRON!"

The airborne science teacher yanked off the apron just as he floated past the flagpole. Then he made a frantic leap for the pole and wrapped his arms and legs tightly about its crowning golden bulb.

The apron rose high into the blue morning sky and soon disappeared among fluffy, white clouds thousands of feet above Middleville.

Freddy gazed out the window at Mr. Wrigglesworth safely wrapped around the swaying flagpole. "Thank heaven he removed that apron!" exclaimed Freddy, with a heavy sigh of relief.

The students stood with shocked faces pressed against the windowpanes, peering in wonder at their teacher, who was screaming and howling high atop the flagpole.

Just then the classroom telephone jingled. Freddy picked up the receiver. "Hello," he said pleasantly.

"Hello. Who is this?" demanded Ms. Torres from her office.

"Freddy Higginbottom, ma'am."

"Well, put Mr. Wrigglesworth on."

"I can't."

"And why not?" demanded Ms. Torres.

"Mainly because he's outside stuck on top of the flagpole," replied Freddy.

"WHERE?" roared the principal.

"On top of the flagpole," repeated Freddy.

Ms. Torres yanked on a white cord to open her Venetian blinds and gazed out her office window at Mr. Wrigglesworth sobbing high atop the flagpole. The dumbfounded principal tore off her glasses and feverishly cleaned the lenses, shook her head as if to clear her faltering brain, and then peered out the office window again. Sure enough, Oliver Wrigglesworth was indeed wrapped about the golden bulb high atop the swaying flagpole. Ms. Torres savagely yanked the cord to snap the blinds shut. "I knew Wrigglesworth would flip sooner or later," she mumbled.

"Ms. Torres, you'd better call a fire truck with a very long ladder," said Freddy over the telephone.

"Thank you and good-bye, Freddy," said Ms. Torres, hanging up the receiver.

The principal sat at her desk for a long while, deeply absorbed in thought. Occasionally she would yank open the blinds, scowl sullenly at Mr. Wrigglesworth screaming hysterically on the bulb, then yank ferociously on the cord to snap the blinds shut again. Finally, she pressed a button on her intercom and called to her secretary: "Ms. Jenkins! Mr. Wrigglesworth is outside on top of the flagpole. Should we call the fire department to rescue him or just leave him up there and dismiss the entire matter?"

"That depends," pondered Ms. Jenkins.

"On precisely *what?*" shouted Ms. Torres into the intercom.

"On whether Freddy Higginbottom is in his science class," replied Ms. Jenkins.

"He *is*," sighed Ms. Torres.

"Then I shall call a fire truck for the poor, unfortunate man," said Ms. Jenkins, dialing the fire department's number.

Ms. Torres sank deep in her leather swivel chair and pressed her fingertips to her throbbing temples. "What will the PTA do when they find out about this?'' groaned the sinking principal.

"And to think that it's only Monday,'' muttered Ms. Jenkins.

Fire sirens wailed in the distance as students streamed from their classrooms and stood in large groups in the schoolyard. Every face gazed skyward at the stricken science teacher marooned on the golden bulb. Inside the school the dazed Charlie Stoots remained sprawled on the lab floor, muttering incoherently to himself.

Just before lunchtime a huge red and silver fire truck groaned to a stop alongside the flagpole. A ladder was

raised, and then a fireman clambered up to the top of the pole and carefully pried the blustering Mr. Wrigglesworth off the golden bulb.

In the science lab Freddy poured a beaker of ice-cold water over the babbling Charlie, shocking him to his senses. Charlie's bleary eyes focused on Freddy. "We did it again, didn't we?" he mumbled groggily.

"I'm afraid so," admitted Freddy, helping Charlie to his feet. "But things could be much, much worse. At this very moment the fire department is rescuing Mr. Wrigglesworth, and it's lucky for us he didn't fly into orbit or something!"

"Yeah, we're really lucky," groaned Charlie. "But, boy-oh-boy, is there going to be trouble when my mother and father hear about this disaster!"

"Come on, Charlie," said Freddy, helping his wobbly friend to the classroom door. "Ms. Torres wants to see us in her office immediately."

"Oh, woe is me!" sighed Charlie.

Freddy helped the weak-kneed Charlie down the long corridor and into the principal's office. From behind her desk, Ms. Jenkins waved the boys ahead to the principal's door. "Go right in, boys," she said. "Ms. Torres is expecting you."

"Don't faint again, Charlie. Whatever you do, don't faint," whispered Freddy, pushing his friend through the door. The two boys stood trembling before Ms. Torres's large, oaken desk.

Ms. Torres slouched sullenly in her swivel chair,

tapping a pencil rhythmically on the desktop. Charlie and Freddy flinched with every tap of the pencil. The principal peered over her glasses at the shaking Freddy and Charlie. "My, my, hasn't this been an exciting morning for you two?" she began.

"Yes, ma'am," replied the boys weakly.

Ms. Torres lurched forward in her chair until her nose was but a single inch from Freddy's face. "Freddy, the school nurse informs me that the shock of being marooned atop that flagpole was too much for Mr. Wrigglesworth. The poor man will be unable to speak for days—maybe even weeks. He's been trundled off to a rest home so that he can gather his shattered wits. So why don't you boys tell me exactly what happened in that science lab this morning, hmmmmm?" she demanded.

"Well, ma'am, it was all sort of an accident," began Freddy. "You see, it all began when Charlie and I decided to make a can of electric paint for the science fair. We mixed all sorts of stuff together and ran it through my Impossible Machine . . . ."

"Your . . . your *what*?" interrupted Ms. Torres.

"Impossible Machine. It performs miracles," said Freddy.

"Proceed with your fairy tale," snapped Ms. Torres.

"Well, ma'am, we sent the paint through the Impossible Machine and out sailed this electric paint, popping and crackling and sputtering like mad." Freddy pulled the bottle of electric paint from his pocket. "At first we thought we could use the paint to make light bulbs out of things, but we

74

were wrong. Instead, we discovered that it frees whatever it touches from the force of gravity. It sent a can of baked beans to the moon.''

"Baked beans with *franks*," interrupted Charlie.

"Yes, franks," added Freddy. "And then we brought the paint to school to show Mr. Wrigglesworth, but he refused to believe in its power and foolishly dabbed a spot of the paint on his apron. After the paint dried, Mr. Wrigglesworth floated out the classroom window and landed on the flagpole. And that's the whole story."

Charlie nodded hopefully.

Ms. Torres rocked swiftly back and forth in her chair. "That story is by far the most preposterous yarn I've heard in all my years as principal of Normal School. And, believe me, I've heard some mighty tall tales in my time!"

"Yes, ma'am," sputtered Freddy and Charlie in unison.

Ms. Torres's swivel chair abruptly lurched to a stop. "Hmmmmmmmmm," she muttered. "Perhaps, just to be on the safe side, you'd better let me have that bottle of paint."

Freddy handed the bottle over the desk to the principal, who immediately walked over to the sink and poured the electric paint down the drain. "There!" she said, returning to her desk. "No more electric paint!"

"May I still do a project for the science fair?" ventured Freddy.

"All right! All right!" sighed Ms. Torres. "But you must promise never to breathe a word of this electric paint business to the PTA."

"We promise!" exclaimed Freddy and Charlie, shuffling out of the office to return to their classes.

The exhausted Ms. Torres shook her puzzled head and then walked over to the sink for a seltzer tablet to settle her queasy stomach. At precisely that moment the electric paint inside the drainpipe dried completely, and before Ms. Torres's bulging eyes, the sink and ten feet of plumbing tore completely out of the wall and floor with a thundering roar of breaking boards and groaning, twisting pipes. The principal stared in horror as the sink and pipes drifted out the office window and high into the air. She ran to the window and watched the sink disappear over the rooftops, then staggered to her desk and fell into her swivel chair. "This can't be happening," she babbled. "It must be my imagination. The strain of this job is finally getting to me. I need a vacation!"

Ms. Torres punched a button on her intercom. "Ms. Jenkins!" she cried.

"Yes, ma'am?" replied Ms. Jenkins.

"Call a plumber immediately and tell him to bring a new sink and ten feet of plumbing pipe. Then book me on the next flight to Honolulu. And don't ask any questions!"

"Yes, ma'am!" replied Ms. Jenkins, shaking her head and dialing the telephone.

A
Clear-Cut
Case of Shell Shock

WHILE THE STUNNED FREDDY and Charlie wobbled on shaky legs back to classes at Normal School, strange things were happening at Freddy's house on Normal Street. Secret Agent Sputterwick marched briskly up the Higginbottom walk armed with a ten-gallon can of heavy-duty motor oil in one hand and a roll of parchment paper in the other. Sputterwick's flowing cape rustled in the mild spring breeze as he stomped up the porch steps and pounded a fist heavily on the front door. He was fiercely determined to crack the Freddy Higginbottom case once and for all. His jaw was firmly set and his very, very beady brown eyes narrowed into slits behind his thick glasses. "I should have gotten around to this weeks ago," muttered Sputterwick, banging on the door again. "Open up in there! I have a warrant to search this house!" he roared.

The door abruptly opened wide to reveal Tremblechin,

standing there with nose blinking on and off, radar-screen eyes flashing brightly, and jaw trembling rapidly.

"Aha!" boomed Sputterwick. "It's you . . . you rusty bucket of bolts. So Freddy Higginbottom has an overgrown pile of tin cans for a butler! Well, I know your weakness, you tinny oil hound," snarled Sputterwick, raising high the ten-gallon can of oil.

The robot saw the can of oil, and his radar-screen eyes lit up like floodlights. Oil-starved cogs and gears deep inside Tremblechin squeaked and whined hungrily, and his tremblechin trembled like a leaf in a hurricane.

Agent Sputterwick poked Tremblechin on his dial-covered chest with the roll of parchment paper. "Go tell Freddy that Secret Agent Sputterwick, the slyest and cleverest of all secret agents, is here with a search warrant to search this house—and make it snappy, tin head."

Tremblechin gathered all his oil pressure and mechanical might to shrug his tin-can arms and shoulders to indicate to the agent that nobody was home except himself.

"Nobody home?" sputtered Sputterwick.

The robot slowly wagged his paint-bucket head.

"Well, no matter," said Sputterwick, unfurling the long roll of paper and handing it over to Tremblechin. "That paper you have there in your tinny little fingers is a search warrant. I'm here to search this house to uncover the secret of Freddy's inventions."

The confused robot stared at the search warrant, and soon the puzzled tin man's radio tubes and electric wires began to overheat and pop and crackle and smoke as the strain of the confusion short-circuited his fuse boxes.

"Now then, why don't you keep yourself busy with this while I search the house," said Sputterwick, handing the huge can of oil over to Tremblechin. "Some tin watchdog! It's easy to outwit a tin man," snarled Sputterwick, bounding into the living room with cape flying.

The contented Tremblechin sat down on the doorstep and sipped oil from the ten-gallon can to sooth his fluttering cogs and gears.

Sputterwick pranced smugly into the deserted Higginbottom house and paused to gaze about the living room. "I'm hot on the trail of Freddy's secrets!" he exclaimed, bounding about the carpet, unsure of just where to begin the search. Then the stubby agent skidded to a stop before the sofa and muttered, "Whoa, George! Whoa! This is your big chance to finally crack this case, so don't get flustered and muff it."

The empty, ten-gallon can clanged on the front porch as Tremblechin drank the last drop of oil, then lay down in the doorway and fell into a deep sleep.

Secret Agent Sputterwick rummaged through the pockets of his cape. "Let's see . . . . ," he sputtered, ". . . handcuffs, bulletproof vest, safety goggles, gas mask, axe, fireproof suit, crash helmet—yep, I'm all ready for the search."

Sputterwick pranced to the cellar door and scrambled down the stairs into the pitch-dark cellar. "I'm hot on the trail! I'm really getting close!" he exclaimed, lighting a match that illuminated clouds of dusty cobweb curtains hanging from the many rows of shelves lining the walls of the musty cellar. Sputterwick held the glowing match close to a row of jars on one of the shelves. "Hmmmmmmmmm . . . raspberry jelly, peach preserves, pickled watermelon rind . . . . Nothing here but canned fruit and vegetables. I sure don't see any miraculous thingamabobs in this dark dungeon. The secret must be upstairs in Freddy's room."

Sputterwick charged up the stairs out of the cellar and scrambled to the stairway leading to the electric room. He stopped short on the first step, realizing that he was about to enter the unknown, and a bolt of fear crackled down his spine and lodged in his knees, causing the joints to knock together loudly. He pulled a tape recorder from his cloak and punched the start button. "Get a grip on yourself, George," he said into the recorder to calm himself. Then he puffed out his chest and crept slowly up the stairs, one trembling step at a time. At the top of the stairs, he stood before Freddy's door and read the sign warning all who entered to wear rubber-soled shoes. He hastily examined the soles of his shoes to make sure they were rubber. With quivering fingers, he reached for the doorknob, twisted it, and threw the door open wide.

"Amazing!" screeched Sputterwick, gazing in awe at the wads of wires, piles of burned-out light bulbs, half-built gadgets, and stacks of electric junk littering the floor, walls, and ceiling of Freddy's room. "It really *is* an electric room!" he marveled, squinting at a charred wad of wires from the last of Freddy's explosions. "From the looks of this junkyard, most of Freddy's inventions must have been bombs,'' muttered the agent into the tape recorder.

Secret Agent Sputterwick tiptoed about the electric room, timidly peeking under piles of junk and snooping under the worktable. ''How in the world can Freddy or anybody else find his way around this electric dump?'' he muttered, peeking under a stack of electric motors. Then the prowling agent wandered to the center of the room, gazed wonderingly about, and clicked on his tape recorder. ''The miracle is here somewhere—I know it. And I'll find it if it takes forever or until lunchtime—whichever comes first!'' he vowed and then switched off his recorder.

Sputterwick had just finished rummaging among Freddy's collection of wrecked radio sets when the closet door caught his eye. His eyebrows raised in surprise and a cold chill came over him as he noticed a faint tinge of light shining under the closet door. ''Eureka!'' he screeched. ''That must be the location of the miracle-maker.'' The trembling agent fumbled in his cloak pockets for his equipment and hastily dressed in a bulletproof vest, crash helmet, safety goggles, fireproof suit, and gas mask. He looked like a being from another planet as he stomped to the closet door and puffed out his chest.

''At long last!'' he exclaimed, yanking open the door to reveal the marvelous Impossible Machine, which rested quietly in the depths of the closet, radiating all the colors of the rainbow. The eerie contraption flamed bright orange and softly beeped and zuzzed and clack-a-ching-chinged. Sputterwick's eyes bulged at the sight of the magnificent impossibility. "So this is the source of all the miracles and disasters," he muttered breathlessly. "Fa-fa . . . fa-fa . . . fantastic!"

The flabbergasted agent stood in front of the closet for several minutes, completely hypnotized by the flowing red, blue, green, yellow, and orange shafts of brilliant light radiating from the Impossible Machine. He flinched every time a wheel or gear on the flaming machine whirred and then quieted itself.

Secret Agent Sputterwick took a hesitant step toward the Impossible Machine but succeeded only in banging a toe sharply on the bucket of electric paint. "Ouch! Ouch! Ouch!" he cried, hopping in circles, clutching his smarting toe. "I should have guessed there would be a booby trap guarding that impossible heap of flames."

The secret agent picked up the mysterious bucket and shook it. Sloshing noises from inside piqued his curiosity, so he carefully popped the lid off the bucket and stared down into the egg-yolk-colored paint. "Looks like a can of liquid electricity," he muttered, sniffing at the contents of the can, "but it smells like pickled eel!"

The nosy agent had no inkling of the paint's mysterious powers, so he carelessly slammed the open bucket down on the worktable, spilling some liquid over the sides, and whirled about to once again face the beaming Impossible Machine. He lifted his crash helmet and scratched his head in wonder. "Now that I've captured the monster, I wonder what to do with it?" Sputterwick whipped a book out of his cloak and anxiously thumbed through the pages.

"Hmmmmmmmmm . . . ," he mumbled, "my spy manual doesn't mention a single thing about what to do with a captured machine such as this."

Suddenly an idea popped into Sputterwick's head. He pulled a pencil and paper from inside his cloak and scribbled:

YOU ARE UNDER ARREST!

Sputterwick's fingers quivered with excitement as he carefully folded the note and placed it on the conveyor belt leading to the Impossible Machine's gaping mechanical mouth. "Take that, you buzz bomb!" he exclaimed, punching the start button.

Agent Sputterwick fled in terror as the Impossible Machine leaped to life. Lights on the monstrous machine flashed brighter and brighter, and wheels, gears, and pulleys whizzed faster and faster. The beeeeep, zuuuzzz, clack-a-ching-ching whined louder and louder until the machine wailed as high as the highest note of a siren. Soon the Impossible Machine shined as brightly as the sun.

Secret Agent Sputterwick swan-dived across the room and sailed under the bed.

The Impossible Machine shook and rattled louder and louder until plaster chips fell from the ceiling, pictures fell from walls, the fireplug on Normal Street sprang a leak, and shingles popped off the roof. Then, quite suddenly, the machine quieted down. The wailing whine softened to a gentle beeeeep, zuuuzzz, clack-a-ching-ching, clack-a-ching-ching, and the brilliant beams of super-light dimmed until the machine once again glowed flaming orange.

The bedazzled agent crawled out from under the bed and scrambled to his feet in front of the Impossible Machine. Sputterwick's eyes bulged behind his safety goggles when out the return chute on the Impossible Machine clattered a shiny, black, metal object the size of an orange that had a sputtering, popping, and smoking fuse protruding from its top.

"Hmmmmmmmmm . . . . ," muttered Sputterwick, delicately picking up the mysterious ball with its wick popping like a Fourth-of-July sparkler, "this daffy machine laid a solid steel egg." He squinted curiously at the little, black globe and scratched his head in wonder. He placed it to his ear and shook it a bit. "Hmmmmmmmmm . . . . ," the agent mumbled, gazing at the sputtering, smoking wick, "come to think of it, this thing looks more like a . . . like a . . . bomb than an egg!" Sputterwick began to panic.

"KA-BOOOOOM!" went the "egg" with a blinding white flash, a geyser of black smoke, and a tremendous force that jolted the entire house.

The clouds of billowing, black smoke slowly cleared to reveal Secret Agent Sputterwick still standing in front of the smugly glowing Impossible Machine, his crash helmet, goggles, and gas mask hanging in shreds around his neck, a thick layer of black soot covering him from head to toe, his tattered, fireproof suit blasted to smithereens, and his cloak hanging in sooty shreds about his shoulders. The tape recorder was a charred wreck and both lenses of Sputterwick's inch-thick glasses were shattered.

The agent stumbled about the electric room as blind as a bat without his glasses. "That was a really good gag!" screamed the enraged Sputterwick. "I couldn't have dreamed up a nastier trick myself!"

The lights on the Impossible Machine twinkled all the laughter of green gems.

"Well, you shall not have the last laugh," snarled Sputterwick, picking up his axe from the floor. "Your puny little bomb failed to destroy my axe." Just as he raised the axe high over his head, preparing to sink the sharp blade into the middle of the Impossible Machine, the sloshed layer of paint inside the bucket of electric paint and the paint that was spilled on the outside dried completely, causing the entire bucket to float up off the table and drift lazily past Sputterwick's nose. The agent slowly lowered his axe and stared cross-eyed at the bucket of paint drifting in midair about the room. Before Sputterwick's disbelieving eyes, the pot of paint sailed out the open window and disappeared high into the blue sky.

"What will happen next in this nuthouse?" gasped Sputterwick, as he once again turned his attention to the Impossible Machine glowing in the closet. "Prepare yourself for the junkyard!" he howled, again raising the sharp axe high over his head. The menacing blade of steel was on a destructive path toward the center of the Impossible

Machine and would have hit its target dead center, had Agent Sputterwick not stepped on a flashlight battery lying on the floor. The battery rolled, turning Sputterwick upside-down in midair. The flying agent landed on a stack of coiled wire and sailed across the electric room atop the rolling coils to the open window. The screaming Sputterwick did a perfect backward swan dive out the second-story window and plummeted like a rock into the fishpond below.

The loud splash and geyser of water issuing from the Higginbottom fishpond caught Officer O'Riley's eye. The officer hastily parked his squad car in front of the Higginbottom house and rushed to the fishpond. There he discovered the sooty, tattered Sputterwick floating on his back in the pond. "Great Scott!" shouted O'Riley, pulling the soggy agent from the pond. "A clear-cut case of shell shock if ever I've seen one!" The officer slapped Sputterwick's face lightly until the tattered agent's sooty eyelids fluttered open.

"Glory be! What happened to you, man? Did you fall from an airplane?" exclaimed O'Riley.

Sputterwick scrambled to his feet and grabbed the officer by his jacket lapels. "Listen!" he roared in O'Riley's face. "An unbelievably brilliant machine just bombed me!"

"Impossible," sputtered O'Riley.

"Please! You must believe me!" wailed Agent Sputterwick. "I arrested the machine in Freddy Higginbottom's closet. The monster beeped and zuzzed and clack-a-ching-

chinged and glowed brighter than the sun until it finally coughed up a bomb and blasted me out the window and into the fishpond.''

"Calm yourself, man!'' demanded O'Riley.

"I AM CALM! I'M AS COOL AS A CUCUMBER!'' roared Sputterwick.

Officer O'Riley towed the protesting agent to the squad car. "Come along now, like a good little man,'' encouraged the officer. "We're going to take a ride down to the station to straighten all this out. After a few days' rest maybe you'll stop telling these impossible fairy tales.'' Then O'Riley gently stuffed the hollering, struggling Sputterwick into the car and buzzed down Normal Street to the police station.

Upstairs in Freddy's closet the Impossible Machine beamed merrily and buzzed joyously. Self-satisfied wheels and gears deep inside the mechanical marvel whirred gaily, and the entire machine blushed a deep shade of flaming crimson as it sensed proudly that it had saved Freddy Higginbottom from the bumbling clutches of Secret Agent Sputterwick.

Meanwhile, Freddy Higginbottom was on his way back to the electric room, where he would soon invent a most extraordinary cookie-crumb-powered motorcar.